Theo Chooses to Help
Th and Ch sounds

FOOD BANKS
GROW COMMUNITIES

By Cass Kim, M.A. CCC-SLP
Illustrated by Kawena VK

D1594946

Theo Chooses to Help
Th and Ch Sounds
P.A.C.B. Speech Sounds Series

This is a work of fiction. Names, characters, places, and incidents either are the product of the author's imagination or are used fictitiously. Any resemblance to actual persons, living or dead, events, or locales is entirely coincidental.

Join us at PACBSpeech.org to find the entire line of books and products!

P.A.C.B.

Phonological and Articulation Children's Books
Learning Speech — Together

Hi! I'm Theo, and today I'm hanging out with my father all day.
His name is Charlie, but I'm not supposed to call him that.
Only adults call him Charlie.

Today is Saturday and, guess what?

Saturday is always a father and son day.
He calls it 'adventure day,' which means we'll be doing chores,
but then we'll get a treat!

A fun thing about my father and I is that we both have an "h" as the second letter in our name.

Except I say mine with a T H, putting my tongue tip between my teeth, and he says his with a C H, pushing his tongue tip up against the roof of his mouth.

You try! Th .....and.....Ch!
Theo and his father, Charlie.

Isn't it weird how the same
letter can sound so different?

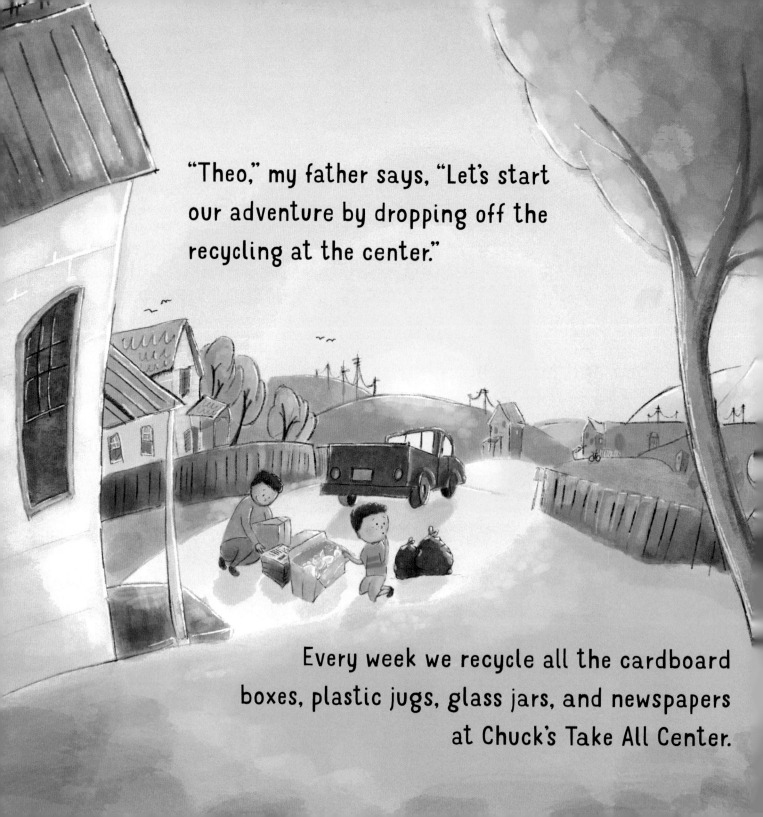

"Theo," my father says, "Let's start our adventure by dropping off the recycling at the center."

Every week we recycle all the cardboard boxes, plastic jugs, glass jars, and newspapers at Chuck's Take All Center.

Father says it's because we are choosing to do good. We could just put them in the garbage, but that's not very good for the Earth.

Once we have all of the recycling loaded into the truck, we head on out.

"Theo," my father says to me, "I want today to be a choice day, not just an adventure day."

"What's a choice day?" This is something we have not done before.

"The kind where you think about making active choices. You're seven now. I want you to look around today and make choices about how to help others."

That could be a really great adventure!
"Cool! What kind of helping?"

"Let's think about that today...there could be many ways to help."

"But can we still get cheesecake, too?" I always get to pick a cheesecake to take home after our chores. It's the best part of the adventure day.

Father chuckles, "You betcha."
I can't wait to see the ways we can help today.

Chuck's Center is bustling and full of people when we arrive.

When we're coming out, a lady approaches us, wearing a tee-shirt that says, "Food Banks Grow Communities." There's a little girl holding a grocery bag next to the words.

"Hi Charlie! Hi Theo!"
It's my teacher, Ms. Champs.
"Hi Miss Champs!" She's a great teacher.

"Have you two heard about the canned food drive for the food bank? This weekend and next, we're asking for donations to support those that need a little extra help right now."

Father takes a flier and nods.
"Thank you, Ms. Champs."

Father puts the flier in his pocket. He doesn't say anything, which is surprising, since he was just talking about making choices to help.

I guess we'll just have to wait and see what other choices we can make today!

At the Post Office, Mr. Tanaka is behind the counter. He's my favorite because he's always smiling, and remembers everybody's name.

Father is stepping up to the counter with his packages when a woman drops her receipt.

Father dashes over and picks up her receipt, then pulls the door open and holds it for her as she is stuffing the paper in her purse.

Her frown immediately turns into a smile,
and that smile makes me smile too.

I think about this as we leave. Even though it was
just a small thing to help that lady, it made
everybody in the post office feel happier.

I like that my father made that choice.

At the gas station, I sit in the car and watch everybody outside while my father fills the tank.

There's a man dropping his chip bag on the ground...but then behind him, another man picks it up and puts it in the garbage can.

I see a woman holding the door for another lady and see as they nod and smile.

A driver honks as a person crosses in front of them, but I see another driver stop and wave for them to go.

Even if not everybody is choosing to be kind... many are. And I want to be like the ones that are helping others.

Our last stop before we head home is Miss Chelsea's Bakery.
Inside, there are so many delicious choices.

She has big birthday cakes that are chocolate or vanilla,
cheesecakes with lime or mango, berries dipped in white
chocolate...and so many cupcakes! There are pastries and
regular cakes and treats of all kinds.

Father always allows me to pick...and I always pick a type of cheesecake.

As I walk along the glass case, peering in at all of the choices, I notice a sticker on the corner by the register. One I've never noticed before.

It's a little girl, holding a bag of groceries. Just like on Ms. Champ's shirt.

FOOD BANKS GROW COMMUNITIES

"Miss Chelsea?"

"Yes, Theo?" She turns from where she's wrapping her famous oatmeal and caramel chunk cookies.

"Do you give canned foods to the food bank?"

Her cheeks lift, and her eyes sparkle.

No, Theo, not usually. But, I do give them some of my
baked goods. That's why we close early on Wednesdays
and Sundays. I take the breads that are still good, but
a day old, and I bring them to food bank to be
distributed with the dinner drop-offs."

"Even the cheesy breads?"

"Even the cheesy breads...when there are any left over.

Those are a best-seller, you know."

"But why don't you just sell them? Or make less?"

"Because I believe that helping others is part of being a community. And it makes me feel like I'm doing something good. People are meant to help each other when they can."

Father nudges me, and I look over and
see an older man with a walker standing
in front of the door. I know that this is a
chance to choose to help.

What should I do?

I should definitely choose to help! I zoom over to open the door. The older man grins at me and rolls slowly into the bakery. It feels good to help.

Now, it's time to choose a treat
and head home for dinner.
Which cheesecake would you choose?
There are so many choices...but
I decide on a chocolate cheesecake.

As we are walking out of Miss Chelsea's Bakery, I have a thought.

"Father? Can we stop at the grocery store on the way home? I think we should get some cans for the food bank."

Father's smile is huge, and he says, "I was hoping you might make that choice."

The End

About the Author: Cass Kim

Cass Kim is an established young adult author. She is best known for creating the "Autumn Nights" Charity Anthology Series, as well as the "Wilders" Young Adult trilogy. In addition to her work as an author, Cass is a practicing Speech-Language Pathologist with a decade of experience. She holds her Certificate of Clinical Competency from the American Speech and Hearing Association, as well as a master's degree from Central Michigan University.

About the Illustrator: Kawena VK

Kawena VK grew up in Hawaii with a great fascination for art and nature. She learned through a traditional atelier at the Windward Community College where she was inspired, by her college instructor, to pursue art. She later received her Bachelor of Arts from the University of Hawaii. With her family and friends, Kawena has found a deep sense of happiness through her love for drawing and painting.

Helpful Tips for Parents:

Th and Ch are both considered digraphs, meaning that two letters come together to form one brand new sound. This makes them slightly trickier than blends when it comes to reading and speech, because sounding out the letters individually just doesn't work. To make it even harder, Th comes in two forms – one with voicing (such as "that"), and one without (such as "thanks"). In English, the voiceless Th is much more common. Ch will always be voiceless, created entirely by the air from our lungs and the movement of our tongue and lips.

To practice voiced vs voiceless sounds, I often have children lightly rest a hand on the front of their throat. First, I have them breathe through their mouth – no vibration is felt in the throat. Then, I have them hum – they should feel the vibration of their voice. This is how I have them test if their voice is "on" for voiced sounds, or "off" for voiceless. They can touch their throat as they practice different words and sounds to feel for "on" or "off" voice.

In this book we take time to highlight how different the 'h' can sound depending on how it is paired. Spending time talking about these differences with kids can help them understand better that sometimes the rules of phonics mean letters can't be sounded out individually, but rather some parings just need to be memorized. Practicing digraphs where children can see the words written out and hear the sound is a great way to work on this. You can make card games from flash cards, such as memory, speed matching, or games like hopping on a sound and saying it.

Here is how I create a memory game: print out 2 cards each that have pictures of words that have the th or ch sound in them (there are word lists on the next pages). We mix them up, flip them upside down, and play the memory game. Taking turns, with every card we flip, we have to say the name – often I'll make it extra silly by pairing a goofy dance move with the different sounds (wiggles for voiced th, sprinklers for voiceless th, and moonwalk for ch). This is a fun way to bring more attention to the targeted sounds.

Sh is another digraph sound. The s and h come to together and create a whole new sound, which makes it different than most of the S+consonant sounds. If your child is struggling with S-blends, or Sh, we have a lot of those sounds in our book "Stephanie's Spectacular Aquarium Visit: S- Blends".

Another way to keep the practice fun and fresh, after you've read this book over and over, is to have them tell you the story back, using the pictures to guide them, or reading it with help for words they get stuck on (depending on age).

Did you know that vision and hearing problems greatly impact speech learning? If your child is struggling to produce sounds, reduced vision or multiple ear infections may be a factor. This is something to bring up to your pediatrician.

These books are not intended to be a substitute for skilled speech therapy treatment. They are meant to be a supplemental addition to practice at home, and a way for families to work together on sound production activities and early literacy skills. If you are concerned about your child's speech, please ask your school system and your pediatrician for a speech therapy evaluation.

Don't forget to stop by our website for free songs and crafts to pair with our P.A.C.B. Speech book series.

Please take a moment to leave a review for this book and the series on Amazon — it makes a big impact for our small business!

FOR MORE INFORMATION ON SPEECH SOUND DEVELOPMENT AND HOW READING IMPACTS SPEECH DEVELOPMENT, VISIT: HTTPS://WWW.PACBSPEECH.ORG/HOME
CHECK US OUT ON INSTAGRAM! @P.A.C.B.SPEECH

Word Lists & Tips

Th is a very visual sound, and you can show it off during practice by putting the tip of your tongue between your teeth. Most children are able to copy this — you can use a mirror or a selfie camera to make it more fun and to help them see what they are doing if they're struggling to copy the movement.

Voiced TH Words — Front of Word:
themselves, therefore, thee, thy, thou

Voiced TH Words — Back of Word:
breathe, seethe, scathe, bathe, loathe, teethe

Voiced TH Words — Middle of Word:
Together, feather, bathing, mother, father, brother, clothing, weather, weatherman, weatherwoman, gather, either, worthy, rather, soothing, teething, smoother, smoothing, leather, other, bother, northern, rhythm

Voiceless TH Words — Front of Word:
the, then, they, there, their, this, them, these, that, though, thorn, thin, think, thunder, thousand, thirsty, thief, theft, thermometer, theater, thermos, thaw, thing, thread, thoughtful, three, thick, thumb, thigh, third, thank you, thirty, thirteen, therapy, Thursday, thimble, thud

Voiceless TH Words — Back of Word:
cloth, moth, math, fifth, beneath, path, month, wreath, booth, broth, ninth, tenth, breath, bath, earth, mouth, teeth, youth, north, strength, south, oath, both, eighth, hath, Ruth, tooth, truth, with, width

Voiceless TH Words — Middle of Word:
athlete, bathtub, toothbrush, python, healthy, truthful, wealthy, toothache, marathon, bathrobe, toothpaste, panther, something, birthday, pathway, toothpick, author, anthem

Ch is a voiceless sound made by our tongue pushing against the roof of our mouth, and our lips rounding. Sometimes I practice by pretending to sneeze and having the children copy my big "a-a-a-choo!" Another trick that works is putting something sticky and yummy (and non-allergy inducing) like a dab of peanut butter or jelly on the roof of the mouth just behind the teeth and having the child place their tongue there to help them find the right place for the tip of their tongue.

CH Words — Front of Word:
chew, chop, chips, choice, choose, chance, chain, champ, chase, cheer, cheek, cheat, chase, chalk, choose, cheese, chick, chicken, chair, child, children, chair, chat, check, chin, cheetah, checkers, cherry, cheeseburger, chili, chocolate, chop, church, chalk, cheap, chipmunk, chore, chapter

CH Word — Back of Word:
touch, each, reach, coach, ditch, ouch, beach, teach, ditch, lunch, which, rich, such, much, pinch, bunch, beach, couch, bench, stretch, pitch, catch, patch, march, touch, speech, wrench, watch, witch, match, branch, switch, ostrich, lunch

CH Word — Middle of Word:
catcher, hatching, crutches, grandchild, ketchup, kitchen lunchbox, inches, matches, marching, touchdown, peaches, picture, itching, pitcher, statue, teacher, witches, furniture, reaching, highchair, temperature, bleachers

Made in United States
Orlando, FL
03 October 2023

37533565R00018